Spooky Sleepover

Sarah
Miles
class
4Y

Follow the Glitter Girls' latest adventures!
Collect the other fantastic books in the series:

Caroline Plaisted

Spooky Sleepover

SCHOLASTIC

Scholastic Children's Books,
Commonwealth House, 1-19 New Oxford Street,
London WC1A 1NU, UK
a division of Scholastic Ltd

London ~ New York ~ Toronto ~ Sydney ~ Auckland
Mexico City ~ New Delhi ~ Hong Kong

Published by Scholastic Ltd, 2002

ISBN 0 439 99458 6

Typeset by Falcon Oast Graphic Art Ltd
Printed and bound in Great Britain by Cox & Wyman Ltd, Reading, Berks

2 4 6 8 10 9 7 5 3 1

Chapter 1

It was Friday afternoon and school was over for the weekend! The Glitter Girls were sitting in Meg's kitchen, busily munching on some pizza slices and debating what they should get up to for their next adventure.

"We could write a book!" suggested Meg. "We could all choose a different character and write about him or her."

"It's OK for you," said Flo, pulling her thumb from her mouth. "You like Creative Writing – and you're good at it. It's harder for people like me."

"And me," Hannah said. "There must be something else we could do."

"And I know exactly what it is!" said Charly.

"There was something in the paper this week about the mayoress's charity – you know, the fund-raising for the town in Africa?"

"Yes, I saw that!" said Zoe, twiddling with the butterfly clip in her hair. "The mayoress wants everyone in the town to help raise money for a children's hospital in Africa. They need to buy some important equipment and medicines."

"Sounds like a good idea – but how can we help?" Flo asked.

"Yes – were there any things in the paper for children to do?" Hannah wanted to know.

"That could be a problem," Zoe said. "Everything I read about was for grown-ups."

"There's got to be something," said Meg, a determined look on her face.

Just then, the back door was flung open and Meg's brother Jack tumbled in, followed by his friend Nick.

"Hi, you lot." Jack dumped his PE kit down by the door and grabbed two glasses from the cupboard. "Got any food?" he asked as he poured some milk into the glasses and handed one of them to Nick.

"Help yourself to some pizza," said Meg, pushing the plate in the boys' direction.

"So, what are you girls up to?" Nick asked the Glitter Girls. Like Jack, he used to go to the same school as the Glitter Girls, so he knew them quite well.

"Just talking and hanging out," said Charly, twiddling with her hair.

"Yes," added Hannah. "We were just wondering what we might get up to this weekend, but we haven't decided yet."

"What are you two doing?" Zoe asked.

"Oh, we're off to the Energy Zone tonight, down at the community centre," Jack explained.

"What's that?" Flo asked.

"It's a youth club," explained Meg. "They go every Monday and Friday night."

"Cool!" said Hannah. "Can we come?"

"No way!" said Nick.

"Why not?" Charly asked. "Can't girls come?"

"No!" said Jack.

"That's not true!" exclaimed Meg. "Sue used to go!"

"So did Jemma and Beth!" added Zoe. "They always had a brilliant time there."

"So why can't we go then?" Flo wanted to know.

Jack and Nick stuffed more pieces of pizza in their mouths and stood leaning against the kitchen worktops, laughing with each other like they were sharing some kind of private joke.

Eventually, Nick said, "Well we just don't want you there tonight."

"Yes – we've got stuff to talk about with Danny," said Jack.

"What stuff?" asked Meg, irritated by her brother.

"And who's Danny?" demanded Charly,

pushing her pink glasses back up on her nose.

"Keep your hair on!" said Jack. "Danny's the bloke that runs Energy Zone."

"What are you going to be talking about?" Meg wasn't going to let her brother get away without explaining why the Glitter Girls couldn't go to the Energy Zone too!

"It's this sleepover," Nick said.

"Sleepover?" the girls exclaimed. They exchanged smiles – a sleepover was definitely something that they wanted to hear about!

"Where are you sleeping over?" Flo wanted to know.

"It's not tonight!" Jack said defensively. "We're just talking about it tonight."

"Well, when is it?" said Meg.

"And where is it?" Hannah quizzed.

"It's in a couple of weeks' time," Nick explained. "In the church tower at St Mildred's."

"Brilliant!" said Zoe.

"Yes," said Jack. "It's going to be cool. We're

doing it to raise money for the mayoress's charity."

"For the African children's hospital!" said Charly.

"How did you know?" Nick exclaimed.

"We read about it in the paper," Hannah said smugly.

"It's a great idea," Meg said, sitting back in her chair with a thoughtful look on her face. "And I don't see why we shouldn't get to do it too!"

"No way!" said Jack quickly, looking to Nick for support.

"Not possible, girls!" added Nick. "You're just too titchy to come."

"How do you know?" said Meg.

Jack and Nick exchanged glances, desperately searching for a reason.

"See!" said Zoe.

"The sleepover's only for members of the Energy Zone," said Jack. "And anyway it's probably full up by now. I'm sure there won't be any space for you lot."

"No," said Nick. "And you'd be too scared!"

"Scared?" Flo exclaimed. "Why? We've done loads of sleepovers!"

"Yes, but not in a church tower!" said Nick.

"A *haunted* church tower," added Jack. "Everyone knows the church has a ghost."

"I've never heard that before," said Flo, secretly wondering if what Jack had just said was true.

"Huh!" said Meg, determined not to be defeated by her brother when a great idea for a Glitter Girl adventure seemed to be within their grasp. "I think that we should go to the Energy Zone ourselves this evening to find out!"

"Go Glitter!" her four friends agreed enthusiastically, only a little bit worried about the thought of the church being haunted.

Jack and Nick looked at each other.

"Oh, *great*. . ." they both sighed.

Chapter 2

With a bit of pleading, the Glitter Girls managed to persuade their parents to let them go to the Energy Zone that night. Jack and Nick weren't at all happy about it.

"It's so uncool," Jack said.

"But there'll be other girls there as well," said Mrs Morgan.

"Not baby sisters though!" Nick muttered, stuffing his hands into his pockets and staring at the floor.

"Look, please just take the girls with you tonight," Mrs Morgan said in her most persuasive voice. "I'm sure they'll keep out of your way. They only want to find out about this sleepover thing. I'll come and collect them when it's over."

"OK, I'll do it this once," groaned Jack, "but I'm not going to take them ever again!"

★ ♥ ★ ♥ ★ ♥ ★

A short while later, the Glitter Girls walked to the Energy Zone with Jack and Nick. They'd decided to go dressed in their favourite Glitter Girl jackets and T-shirts. That way everyone at the Energy Zone would know who they were.

"I don't know why you're bothering," said Nick. "There won't be any spaces left on the sleepover anyway." He and Jack were trying to walk along in front of the Glitter Girls as if they weren't really with them.

"And you'd be scared stiff," said Jack, turning his head to speak to them. "You girls couldn't cope with all that howling. The church tower ghost is a great howler."

"How do you know about the ghost?" Hannah asked.

"Yes – I don't know anyone that's ever seen or heard of it!" agreed Zoe.

"Well. . ." Jack was lost for words. "I just do – everyone knows!"

"It sounds like some silly story to me," said Flo, as they finally arrived at the hall.

"Yes," hissed Meg. "And I wouldn't be at all surprised if my brother's made the whole thing up!"

The girls followed Jack and Nick inside and were immediately met by a tall man clutching a clipboard.

"Who have we got here then?" he said, smiling at them.

The Glitter Girls introduced themselves.

"They've only come to find out about the sleepover," Jack explained.

"And we've told them that there isn't any point because they're too young to come and it's full anyway," Nick added.

"We'll have to see about that," said the man.

He turned to the Glitter Girls. "My name's Danny, and I run the Energy Zone. It's good to meet you all. In fact, you aren't too young to come on the sleepover – as long as your parents don't mind, of course, but I'm not sure that we've got space for you all. I think we're nearing our limit of twenty people."

"Ohh!" the girls all sighed at once. The sleep-over had sounded like such a good idea.

Danny smiled at the girls. "But let's see what happens tonight, shall we? Everyone's going to confirm this evening if they can come or not."

The Glitter Girls nodded and looked around the hall. There were a lot of children already there, waiting for the Energy Zone to begin. If Danny only had space for twenty people on the sleepover, it didn't look too hopeful.

A few minutes later, everyone was seated in the middle of the hall.

"Hi guys," Danny said. "I just want to talk to you all quickly about the sleepover. So – hands up who's coming with us in a fortnight's time?" Danny asked.

There was a flurry of fidgeting and then what looked like a sea of hands went up. Danny started to count them.

"Sixteen . . . seventeen . . . erm, that's everyone." Danny wrote something down on his clipboard.

Meg gulped and looked at her friends. Seventeen? That meant that there were only three spaces left. But there were five Glitter Girls – too many to go on the sleepover! They were so disappointed – what had seemed like a great adventure was no longer going to happen. The Glitter Girls sat, twiddling their fingers and picking at their trainers as Danny wrote down the names of everyone who had put up his or her hand. He stared down at his clipboard looking a little confused. The girls looked on in silence, as Danny began counting the names on his list under his breath.

"Fourteen . . . fifteen. . ." Danny stopped, looking puzzled. "Hang on a minute, I thought I counted seventeen hands, but I've only got fifteen names here!"

Danny scratched his head. Jack and Nick sat giggling behind the Glitter Girls, laughing at some private joke.

They're probably laughing because we're not coming, thought Meg.

"OK, you lot, call out your names!" called Danny and he started to tick the names off against the list he'd written.

Jack and Nick were sniggering so much that Danny had to tell them to be quiet at one point.

When Danny'd finished counting up the names again, he said, "OK – who's mucking about? I've still only got fifteen names here."

By now, Jack and Nick were laughing uncontrollably.

"It's you two, isn't it?" Danny said, smiling himself now. "You each put up two hands, didn't you?"

Jack and Nick carried on laughing. Obviously Danny was right.

"Very funny, you nearly had me there. Right, it looks as if fifteen of you are coming on the sleepover then," Danny said. Then he turned to the Glitter Girls and said, "Which means that if you girls can get your parents' permission – and lots of sponsorship of course – you can come with us!"

"Go Glitter!" they all replied at once!

"No way!" groaned Jack and Nick. . .

★ ♥ ★ ♥ ★ ♥ ★

Later on, Danny handed out sponsorship forms for the sleepover. There was also another sheet that explained the sort of kit that people needed to bring with them for the night – sleeping bags, warm clothes and stuff. It included a picnic so that they could have a midnight feast!

"Doesn't it sound cool?" Charly asked.

"Yeah, brilliant!" said Zoe.

"We should have a meeting," said Meg. "To get ourselves organized!"

"Yes, but we haven't asked our parents yet, have we?" said Hannah. "What happens if they won't let us go?"

"Well, we'll just have to make them let us go!" said Meg resolutely.

Chapter 3

The Glitter Girls nagged their parents all weekend – they had to go on the sleepover!

"I promise I'll keep my room really tidy!" Flo told her mum and dad.

"I'll do my homework everyday without even being asked!" Zoe said to hers.

"I'll let Lily play with my things!" Charly offered.

"I'll wash the car!" Hannah said to her parents.

"I promise I'll keep out of Jack's way once the sleepover's finished," Meg promised her mum.

Eventually, after the Glitter Girls had promised that they would indeed do all the things they had said they would, and their parents had discussed it with one another, the girls got an answer. Their parents said yes! The Glitter Girls *were* going on the sleepover!

★ ♥ ★ ♥ ★ ♥ ★

On Monday, after school, the Glitter Girls met up at Charly's house to begin their preparations.

"Tea in half an hour, girls, OK?" Mrs Fisher said as Meg, Charly, Flo, Hannah and Zoe arrived and headed upstairs.

"Thanks, Mrs Fisher!" they called. They settled themselves in Charly's room and Meg pulled out her notebook.

"So," said Meg, "has everyone looked at Danny's list? Is there anything we need to take that's extra special?"

"No," Charly replied. "It's all the usual stuff."

"So what else can we take to make it fun?" Meg asked.

"Walkmans!" said Zoe.

"Lots to eat!" exclaimed Hannah.

"Make-up!" suggested Flo.

"I don't suppose there'll be much time to do any makeovers," said Hannah. "And don't forget there'll be boys there – they'll probably make fun of us if we take make-up!"

"Who cares what they think!" said Zoe. "Still, you've got a point, Hannah – we'd better make sure that we're prepared for them!"

"How are we going to do that?" Charly wanted to know.

"I can tell you haven't got a brother," Meg said. "But I know what Jack's like – he's bound to get up to something. Something totally stupid probably – and I bet he and Nick will try and scare us."

"What sort of thing do you think they might do?" Hannah felt a bit nervous. She had a younger brother and he was a bit stupid sometimes but he'd never done anything really bad. . .

"Oh, don't worry about it," Meg said reassuringly. "They'll probably just try to play tricks on us. And I'll probably be able to find out *what* tricks. . ."

"How?" asked Zoe.

"Just because they're boys!" Meg laughed. "And boys are idiots – and they can't keep secrets!"

The Glitter Girls all laughed.

"OK, what else shall we take?" Meg asked, looking down at her notebook.

The Glitter Girls spent the next few minutes deciding which CDs they'd take, what they wanted in their midnight feast and what night-wear they'd need.

"Well, that's that sorted then," said Meg, ticking everything off on her list. "Now – sponsorship!"

"I think we need to do something bigger than just asking everyone we know," Flo suggested.

"Yes," agreed Zoe. "Anyway, everyone else at

the Energy Zone will be doing that, won't they?"

"I know, why don't we go along to the newspaper office?" Charly said. "Maybe we could persuade them to write an article about us or something!"

"Good idea!" said Flo.

"Only problem with that though," said Meg, tucking her long wavy hair behind her ears, "is that the paper is already asking people in the town to send in money for the mayoress's appeal, isn't it?"

"That's true," said Hannah. "So they might not be that interested."

The Glitter Girls sat in silence, each of them trying to come up with a brilliant suggestion that would bring them loads of sponsorship.

"Got it!" Zoe shouted so loudly that the others jumped.

"What?" Meg asked.

"Radio!" Zoe looked very pleased with

herself. "Mum told me that Suzy's left the hospital radio station and now she's working at the local radio station."

When the Glitter Girls had had their very own radio show at the hospital where Zoe's mum worked, Suzy had helped them produce Glitter FM. She'd been so nice – surely she'd help them out again now she was presenting a programme for the local station?

"Fantastic!" the remaining Glitter Girls said.

"Do you think Suzy would be interested in the sleepover, then?" Charly asked.

"We can ask her," suggested Meg, writing it down on her list of things they had to do.

"Yeah, let's see if Suzy can mention the sleep-over on her next programme!" suggested Zoe.

"Great idea!" said Flo. "But we'd better tell Danny about it first, don't you think?"

"She's right," said Hannah. "We do need to check it out with Danny."

"But do you think we need to find out if Suzy

wants to do something about it first?"

"Hmm," Meg put her pencil thoughtfully in her mouth. "Good point. . . Could you ask your mum to phone Suzy, Zoe? Then we can suss it out with her before we talk to Danny."

"Yeah, sure," Zoe said, nodding. "I'll talk to her tonight."

"Go Glitter!" everyone yelled enthusiastically.

★ ♥ ★ ♥ ★ ♥ ★

On the Friday night, Nick and Jack went into another big sulk about taking the Glitter Girls with them to the Energy Zone.

"Oh *no*, not again, Mum! I said I'd take them once, but that was it. I can't believe I have to have my sister and all her dumb friends tag along with us – it's embarrassing," Jack whinged when his mum told him that the girls would be going with him and Nick.

"Oh, stop moaning, Jack. It's not like anyone else will notice!" Mrs Morgan said. "And please don't be so unkind about your sister and her friends."

"But Mrs Morgan," Nick sighed, "do we have to? Girls are so stupid. . ."

"I think that's enough thank you," Mrs Morgan snapped at the two boys. "You're taking them – no more arguing!"

Nick and Jack moaned at the Glitter Girls all the way to the Energy Zone.

"I hope you girls aren't going to be all embarrassingly scared when the headless ghost appears in the graveyard," Nick said, as they turned into the road where the hall was.

"Course not," said Zoe, thinking quickly. "We'll be safely inside the church tower, won't we? Not in the graveyard!"

Flo laughed. "Yeah, we'll be fine!"

"Course, they say there are lots of other ghosts in the church too," Jack said casually.

"Rubbish!" said Charly, not sounding too convinced.

"Well," Nick smirked. "I'm sure you'll get scared at the sleepover anyway."

"Why would we?" Hannah asked suspiciously.

Nick and Jack were sniggering and looking slyly at each other. The Glitter Girls could tell they were up to something.

"Oh – I should think," Jack said, stifling a giggle, "that the sleepover will be a night to remember, that's all."

The Glitter Girls looked at each other conspiratorially. They didn't have to say anything to each other but they all knew that they weren't going to be tricked by two daft boys.

By this time they'd arrived at the hall, and there was no more time to talk.

The Energy Zone was packed that night and the Glitter Girls only just managed to find seats next to each other. They hadn't been sitting down for long when Danny greeted them all. He told everyone that they were going to do a sponsored car wash at the supermarket in town the next Saturday.

"I'll provide the buckets and sponges," Danny told them. "The supermarket's giving us the water and soap and you lot need to bring your waterproof clothes and wellies! Hands up who can come?"

Danny jotted down the names of the boys and girls with their hands up. Jack and Nick had volunteered too – in fact, they were helping to organize it.

"So," said Danny, flopping down on to the only empty chair left. "Tell me all about your sponsorship plans, everyone!"

The other boys and girls at the meeting told Danny about the members of their family that were going to sponsor them. Along with their neighbours and teachers and others, it sounded like quite a lot of sponsors.

"So – has anyone else got any other ideas for sponsorship?" Danny asked the crowd sitting around the hall.

Meg put up her hand and told Danny all

about the idea that the Glitter Girls had had that afternoon.

"My mum rang Suzy for us," Zoe said. "She knows us, you see. And Suzy said that she liked the sound of the idea if you were keen, Danny."

"Sounds great to me – it'd be excellent publicity," Danny smiled. "What does everyone else think?"

Danny looked around at all the other boys and girls and they all shouted their approval.

"Well then, girls – can you ask Suzy to get in touch with me? I'm sure we can sort something out. . ."

"Go Glitter!" the girls called back.

Chapter 4

As soon as the meeting was over, the Glitter Girls started chatting away about their brilliant idea.

"We need to phone Suzy and tell her," Meg said.

"Good idea," said Zoe. "It's a bit late now, but why don't we call her tomorrow after school?"

"Go Glitter!" came the reply from her friends.

★ ♥ ★ ♥ ★ ♥ ★

When the girls got back to Charly's house after school the next day, Charly asked her mum if they could phone Suzy.

"Which one of us should talk to her?" Hannah wondered aloud. "Meg?"

"Well actually, with our phone all five of you could just about manage to speak to Suzy at once – you can press the speaker button and talk to her without using the receiver!"

"Brilliant!" said Charly. "Thanks, Mum!"

"Yes – thanks, Mrs Fisher!" the others all said.

Zoe dialled the number her mum had written down for her.

Meg spoke first and explained that Danny was as keen as the Glitter Girls to have the sleepover mentioned on her next programme.

Suzy was really pleased, and she had some even better news for the Glitter Girls. She'd spoken to her colleagues at the radio station and it had been decided that she should do more than just mention the sleepover – they thought Suzy should get *really* involved!

"Well, there's going to be a meeting of the Energy Zone on Friday night at the church – so we can make our final plans," Meg told her.

"Is there? Hmm . . . I think I ought to be

there," Suzy said. "I'm covering the African month on my programme so any more information I can record this week can be included – it'll all help to get people in the town enthusiastic."

"Great!" said Flo.

"Will we be interviewed?" Charly asked.

"Probably – I'd like to record as many of you as possible," Suzy confirmed. "OK, well Dr Baker gave me Danny's phone number so I'm going to give him a call to check the arrangements with him."

"Cool!" Meg said.

"But in the meantime, can you girls give me some more information about the sleepover? How many of you are going to be doing it, and that sort of thing?" Suzy asked.

Between them, the five best friends told Suzy everything that had already been planned for the sleepover.

"Well, let's hope that we can get all of our

listeners to sponsor you," Suzy said.

The Glitter Girls giggled in approval and anticipation.

"Right, hopefully I'll see you on Friday, girls. Bye!"

"Bye Suzy!" the girls all said together.

★ ♥ ★ ♥ ★ ♥ ★

The Glitter Girls were so excited about Friday night that it was a struggle to concentrate on anything else. But eventually Friday afternoon came and the girls raced back to their rooms to change into their Glitter Girl jackets and jeans. As soon as they'd had their tea, they zoomed off to meet in Meg's bedroom.

"Do you think we'll be scared?" Flo wondered; she'd been worrying about what Jack and Nick had said earlier in the week. "You know – of the ghost?"

"There is no ghost!" said Meg. "It's just something my stupid brother has made up!"

"Course there isn't!" Hannah echoed, not at all sure that she felt as confident as Meg did.

The others remained silent. Supposing there really was a ghost? Were Jack and Nick really clever enough to make something like that up? A sponsored sleepover was fun – but a spooky sponsored sleepover wasn't the same thing at all. . .

"Look," Meg said, sensing her friends' fear, "Jack and Nick are probably plotting some joke – if we're ready for it, it won't work, will it?"

"No way!" agreed Zoe. "So what are we going to do about it?"

But before Meg could answer, her brother knocked on her door and grumpily told them it was time to walk to the Energy Zone. His mum had forced him into it again, and he wasn't very happy!

"We'll talk about it another time," Meg whispered.

★ ♥ ★ ♥ ★ ♥ ★

"Hi, girls! Hi, Jack!"

Suzy was already at the hall when Jack, Nick and the Glitter Girls arrived. She had been deep in conversation with Danny when they walked in.

"Hello, Suzy!" the girls all said at once. "Hi, Danny!"

"I've just been hearing some more details about this sleepover of yours," Suzy smiled. "It sounds fantastic fun."

"Yes!" Danny said with a very pleased grin on his face. "Suzy's coming with us tonight to check out the church tower."

"Definitely," said Suzy. "And we can start tonight. I thought we'd record something about the sleepover at the church tower – you know, telling the listeners exactly what's involved and asking them to sponsor you all. . ."

"Great!" exclaimed Charly, and the others nodded in agreement.

"Right, you lot!" Danny called to everyone at the Energy Zone. "Let's get our act in gear and set off for the church!"

★ ♥ ★ ♥ ★ ♥ ★

It didn't take long to get to the church, which was positioned just off the high street. It was just beginning to get dark as they arrived and the huge, spooky old trees that stood in the graveyard were rustling in the wind.

Instinctively, the Glitter Girls huddled closer to each other as they walked up the long path that weaved its way through the tombstones to the church itself.

When they got to the door, they waited while Danny fished in his pockets for the key.

"Hey, did you see that?" Nick said.

"What?" Zoe asked, looking quickly over her shoulder towards Jack and Nick.

"Something moved behind that gravestone!" Jack whispered.

"Where?" Hannah, Flo and Charly said at once.

Meg, who knew her brother well and could see that Nick was trying to conceal a grin, said, "Take no notice of them! They're having us on! There's nothing there."

"Found it!" said Danny, taking a key from his pocket and turning it in the lock. "Let's go."

It was very dark inside the church and the Glitter Girls were still grouped together protectively. Danny soon found the light switches and flicked them on to reveal nothing unusual – just the church that the Glitter Girls recognized from the occasional school concert. It was funny how different it had felt in the dark.

"So who's been up in the tower before, then?" Danny asked, making his way towards a door by the side of the vestry.

Nobody answered.

"Right," said Danny. "Well – follow me."

He found another light switch and started to wend his way up the steep steps, closely followed by the rest of the sleepover team.

"Hey – there's a lot of cobwebs up here!" Flo whispered to her friends.

"Do you think there are any bats?" Hannah asked.

"Shouldn't think so," Charly said.

"But there might be some spiders!" Meg hated spiders.

"Don't worry – we'll protect you if there are," Flo reassured her.

Zoe was too busy counting the steps up to the top of the tower to join in until she said, "Hey – 134! Phew! It's a long way up!"

"So," said Danny, opening a door at the top. "This is where we're going to sleep over! It's cool, isn't it? It used to be the vicar's study until they made room for one downstairs."

The Glitter Girls looked round the room. There was still a desk and some chairs, as well as some bookshelves. The carpet was really old and had bald patches on it. On the one side there were two windows, hung with thin curtains. Against the walls were some old bookcases, but instead of books, there were tatty cardboard boxes lining some of the shelves.

"You'll be glad to know that there is a storage heater in here," Danny said, shivering. "And it will be switched on for us!"

It was actually quite a big room and not nearly as scary as some of the Glitter Girls had begun to fear it would be.

Danny went on to explain to everyone exactly how they would lay out the sleeping bags with girls on one side and the boys on the other. "You can see right down into the graveyard," said Jack, looking out of one of the windows.

"So what?" said Meg, determined not to be rattled by her brother.

After everyone had done a bit of exploring, Suzy asked for quiet so that she could interview

Danny for the programme. After she'd recorded him talking, Suzy went on to ask some of the children questions about the mayoress's charity and their involvement in the sleepover. Then she asked the Glitter Girls about the sponsorship and recorded Charly saying, "It's really spooky up here! Please can everyone send as much money as they can to help pay for the new equipment that they need at the hospital? Then we can get out of here!"

"That was terrific – thanks, guys," said Suzy, switching off her tape recorder.

"Come on, everyone," Danny said. "Let's get going."

Danny switched off the light and everyone began to climb back down the stairs. Suddenly, there was a terrible crash from the other side of the tower room!

The Glitter Girls froze on the stairs. Maybe Jack and Nick were right about the ghost after all!

Chapter 5

"What was that?" shrieked Zoe.

The Glitter Girls grabbed each other, too terrified to speak and too scared to peer through the gloom back into the tower room. In the dim light, even Jack and Nick looked frightened.

"Don't worry!" Danny said, as he quickly reached for the light switch.

The room was illuminated once more, but no one said a word and the air was eerily still as Danny walked tentatively across the room.

He let out a sigh. "It's OK, everyone!" he said, almost laughing with relief. "It's only a piece of wood that's fallen over in the corner here! It knocked into one of the boxes on the shelves and threw the contents all over the floor – that's why the noise was so loud."

"Phew!" said Meg.

"I thought it was the ghost!" sighed Flo.

"Me too!" added Zoe, Flo and Hannah.

"I told you before," said Meg. "Jack's just made it up! There is no ghost."

"Actually," whispered Zoe. "He looked just as scared as us!"

The Glitter Girls giggled. The sleepover was going to be great fun!

The Glitter Girls didn't take part in the car wash the next day but when they met up at school on Monday morning, Meg told them that Jack had reported that they'd raised nearly a hundred pounds.

"That's fantastic!" said Zoe, and the others agreed.

"I can't wait to hear Suzy's programme tonight," said Charly.

"I wonder if she'll mention the car wash as well as the sleepover?" Hannah mused.

Just then the bell went, signalling the end of break, and the girls headed back to their classrooms.

★ ♥ ★ ♥ ★ ♥ ★

". . .So all you listeners out there – please make sure that you sponsor the Energy Zone boys and girls for their sleepover next week! You can send your donations to the radio station and we'll be happy to pass the money on! And now it's time for the news. . ."

The Glitter Girls were in Charly's bedroom.

"That was great, wasn't it?" said Charly, switching the radio off. "She gave us a really good plug!"

"If that doesn't get us loads of sponsors, I don't know what will!" Hannah exclaimed.

"It was fantastic!" said Zoe, and the others nodded in agreement.

"Now that the sponsorship's well under way, we need to get ourselves organized for Saturday's sleepover," said Meg.

"My family's got loads of sleeping bags so I'll bring a few extra," said Flo.

"I'll get some CDs together," said Zoe. "I'm sure Jemma and Beth will let me borrow some of theirs as well."

"I can bring my CD player," Charly added. "It's really tiny so it won't take up much space in my backpack."

Meg was busy writing all these things down. "What kind of clothes do you reckon we should take?" she wondered aloud.

"It's probably best to wear jeans or tracksuit bottoms or something," suggested Hannah. "I mean, the church tower isn't the sort of place for skirts, is it?"

"No, it was pretty dusty!" agreed Zoe. "But

we'll need our nightclothes too, won't we?"

"Yes," said Meg. "And we'd better make sure they're warm ones, too."

"Good idea," Charly agreed, remembering the chilly, dark room.

"That's if we get any sleep!" giggled Flo, thinking of the Glitter Girls' usual sleepovers. No one had slept very much, but everyone had had a really great time!

The others laughed.

"I wonder if Suzy will come and visit us when we're doing the sleepover?" Zoe said.

"Hey, that would be great, wouldn't it?" Hannah sighed.

"Yeah, it would! I think we should ask Danny about it on Friday night at the Energy Zone, don't you?" suggested Charly, pushing her pink glasses back up on her nose.

The other girls nodded in agreement.

"Now," said Meg, looking back at her notebook. "What are we going to take for our midnight feast?"

"Danny said that we had to bring stuff that didn't need heating up," reminded Hannah.

"And that it was best to bring things that we could share," added Charly, who was plaiting her hair as she spoke.

"I'll bring some Chinese fortune cookies," said Flo. "As well as some Coke."

"I'll make some mini-quiches with my mum," said Meg.

"I'll bring mini-chocolate rolls and one of those really big bags of mixed sweets!" Hannah decided.

"How about I bring some crisps and some little cartons of juice?" Zoe suggested.

"Good idea," said Charly. "I think I'll bring some sandwiches and some popcorn."

Meg finished writing in her notebook and said, "Now – what shall we bring to sort out Jack and Nick?"

Flo laughed. "Do you really think they're up to something?"

"I'm certain of it!" said Meg. "They've made it clear that they're still not happy about us being at the sleepover, haven't they?"

"And they're always whispering and giggling whenever we see them. . ." sighed Zoe.

"And I'm sure I heard Jack on the phone talking to Nick about some kind of trick last night," confirmed Meg.

Charly looked decidedly worried. "Do you think we're going to be OK?"

Meg gave her friends a knowing smile. "Course we are! I've just had a very good idea," she said. "A very good idea indeed!"

"What?" the others wanted to know.

"Last Christmas, my aunt gave Jack a whole box of tricks – you know, fake biscuits, soap that makes your skin dirty, that sort of stuff," Meg explained. "And my mum got so fed up with Jack catching her out that she confiscated the tricks and hid them. Only *I* know where she hid them. . ."

". . .So you're going to bring them with you to the sleepover!" Zoe guessed.

"Exactly!" laughed Meg.

"Brilliant!" said Hannah.

"Then we can get our own back," confirmed Flo.

"If we need to – yes!" said Meg.

"Girls?" Mrs Fisher called up the stairs. "It's time for tea!"

"Great!" said Charly. "All this talk about food's made me hungry!"

"Well, I think that's everything sorted," said Meg, snapping her notebook shut. "All we've got to do now is hope that Suzy's programme gets a good response and then we're ready for action on Saturday!"

"Go Glitter!"

Chapter 6

At Friday's Energy Zone, the first thing Danny did was congratulate everyone who'd been involved in the sponsored car wash at the weekend.

"We had a totally sloppy and soapy time and managed to raise about a hundred pounds!"

There were cheers all round.

"The supermarket was so impressed with us that they've said we can come back another time if we want. And. . ." Danny paused dramatically, ". . .they've offered to match that hundred pounds if we do the sleepover tomorrow!"

Some of the boys whooped and everyone started to clap.

"Well done to everybody who was involved. Now, are you lot ready for tomorrow night?" Danny asked.

"Yessss!" came the enthusiastic reply.

"Great!" said Danny, as excited as they were. "OK, we're going to meet up at the church at seven o'clock tomorrow evening. Everyone should know what they've got to bring. . ."

There were mumbles of confirmation all around.

". . .basically anything that *you* want to scoff and some more of whatever it is to share around with everyone else. You'll also need your sleeping bag and nightclothes and lots of jumpers to keep you warm. So has anyone got any problems with that?"

"Nooooo, Danny!" everyone replied.

"Any questions then that anyone wants to ask?" Danny looked around the room at all of their eager faces.

Meg put her hand up with lightning speed.

"Yes, Meg?" Danny smiled at her.

"We know that Suzy has mentioned the sleep-over a lot on the radio," Meg said. "And we wondered if she might be able to come along tomorrow night?"

There were mumbles of approval from the others in the room.

Danny beamed at Meg and the other Glitter Girls.

"Well – thanks mostly to the Glitter Girls – Suzy has already been in contact with me this week," Danny confirmed. "She wanted to let us know that we've had lots of people pledge to sponsor us and the Africa month in general."

Everyone cheered.

"*And*," Danny continued, when the noise level lowered again, ". . .Suzy will be coming along tomorrow night to have a chat with us. In fact, she's going to join us for the whole night – she's going to sleep over too!"

The Glitter Girls cheered loudly – they were

so pleased Suzy would be with them on the sleepover.

Danny waved his hands, gesturing at everyone to quieten down so that he could tell them something else.

"Quiet, you guys!"

Eventually everyone was.

"OK! Now – the final bit of news! Not only is Suzy joining us for the sleepover, but she's going to broadcast some live stuff from the church tower tomorrow. You're all going to be famous!" Danny said, laughing. "Suzy's going to do five-minute stints throughout the evening and you lot will be interviewed."

Now the roof nearly came off! Danny had to gesture again to make everyone quieten down.

"Go Glitter!" the Glitter Girls screamed with excitement. And this time, everyone else in the hall joined in! Except Jack and Nick, who Meg spied muttering and laughing to each other over on the other side of the hall.

"Those two are definitely up to something!" Meg said, nudging Zoe who was sitting next to her.

"Well maybe they'll be in for a shock when we get our own back!" Zoe said, trying to stifle a giggle before anyone else saw.

★ ♥ ★ ♥ ★ ♥ ★

It was six o'clock on Saturday night, and the Glitter Girls had arranged to meet at Zoe's house, so that her dad could give them a lift to the church. RAT tat tat! went the knock on Zoe's bedroom door.

"Who is it?" Zoe whispered.

"GG!" came the reply and Zoe opened the door, not at all surprised to see her four best friends standing on the landing.

"Come in!" she said, smiling.

All five of them were wearing groovy trousers in various shades of denim, pink and purple. Meg's were tie-dyed with fantastic patterns on them and the others had sequins and embroidery on theirs.

"Everyone got all their stuff?"

Meg ticked everything off her list and closed her notebook. She looked at her pink bubble watch. "Well – that means that we've got forty-five minutes to get ourselves ready then!"

"Cool!" said Charly. "Who's going to braid my hair?"

"I'll do it!" Zoe volunteered. "As long as someone will do mine!"

"We could stand in a ring and do everyone's hair at the same time!" suggested Flo.

"Good idea!" said Meg, and that was exactly what the Glitter Girls did.

After braiding, plaiting and threading beads into each other's hair, the Glitter Girls turned to their nails. It was impossible to do nails in a ring so in the end they all decided to paint their own and then they took turns to decorate each other's nails with transfers and diamanté.

"Right," said Zoe, when their nails were dry. "I make it quarter to seven. I reckon we should think about leaving."

At almost exactly the same time, there was a knock on Zoe's door.

"Girls?" It was Mr Baker. "Are you ready? We'd better go!"

The Glitter Girls giggled.

"Perfect timing!" said Hannah.

The Glitter Girls all put their denim jackets on.

"Coming, Dad!" Zoe called, walking over and opening the door.

Mr Baker smiled at the five friends. "Go Glitter?" he asked them.

"Go Glitter!" they confirmed.

Chapter 7

Some of the others were already there when the Glitter Girls arrived at the door of the church.

"Hello there!" said Danny, ticking the five girls off on his list. "Only a few more to go before we're all here."

"Is Suzy here yet?" Charly asked.

"Yes, she's upstairs already – getting her recording equipment set up," Danny explained. "Jack and Nick are up there helping her – do you lot want to go on up too?"

"Too right!" said Flo. "Bye, Mr Baker!"

"Bye, Dad!" Zoe kissed her father.

"Yes, bye!" called the others. "Thanks for the lift!"

"Have a good time, girls! And watch out for the ghost!" Mr Baker smiled and set off back down the path through the graveyard.

Zoe looked at the tombstones that surrounded them. Some of them were very old and leaning to one side. The light was fading fast and the moon could just be seen hiding behind the church tower. Zoe shivered as she wondered if Jack's ghost story was true.

"Zoe?"

Zoe turned to see Meg calling her.

"Are you coming?" Meg asked. "We're going up to see Suzy."

"Course!" said Zoe, following her friends. But just as she got to the church door, she could have sworn that she saw something moving behind one of the trees. "What was that?" she said anxiously.

"What?" Flo asked.

"Something moved!" Zoe said. "Behind the trees!"

"Where?" Hannah asked, looking across the graveyard.

Zoe pointed in the direction of what she'd seen.

"You mean those two boys?" Meg asked, as the Glitter Girls watched some of the stragglers coming through the graveyard to join them.

"Oh yes!" Zoe sighed with relief. Suddenly she felt really silly. "Come on – let's go and see Suzy!"

Jack and Nick had nearly finished sorting things out with Suzy by the time the Glitter Girls had climbed all those steps and joined them in the tower room.

"Well, hello, girls!" Suzy smiled as she greeted them.

"Hi, Suzy! Is there anything we can do?" Meg asked, looking around at the technical equipment Suzy had started to set up.

"Just watch out for the ghost!" Jack warned.

"Haroooooo!" howled Nick before he and Jack dissolved with laughter at their own joke.

"Very funny," sighed Meg, winking at the other Glitter Girls.

By now it was almost pitch black outside as the last of the other boys and girls found their way up the gloomy staircase.

"Right," said Danny, putting his own rucksack down on the floor. "I think we're all here. Everything OK, Suzy?"

"Fine, thanks!" Suzy smiled and looked at her watch: it was twenty past seven. "Right, we've got a slot on the radio in ten minutes. I'm going to need you all to be really quiet when I'm recording. Is that OK with everyone?"

"I'm sure it is," said Danny. "We can do that, can't we?"

"Yes!" everyone called back.

"Right then." Danny began to get everyone organized. "Put your backpacks and all your gear down here, please. Then everyone sit down and wait quietly for the action to begin."

Soon everyone was sitting in a circle on the floor. The air was buzzing with excitement. Suzy explained that they couldn't listen to the show on their Walkmans and radios because it would make feedback noises on the programme once they were on air. But as she tuned everything in and twiddled knobs on the recording equipment, they were able to hear the programme loud and clear anyway.

"...Now regular listeners will remember that last week we heard about a special sleepover that's happening in town tonight. The boys and girls from the Energy Zone are being sponsored to raise funds for the improvements to the hospital in the African town which has been the focus of the mayoress's charity. Amongst the kids at the Energy Zone are the Glitter Girls, who kindly let us know about what they're getting up to tonight. And we're delighted to tell you that lots of you have already sent in your pledges to support the kids as they sleep over.

"Our intrepid reporter and presenter Suzy has joined the Energy Zone this evening and, any second now, we should be hearing live from the church tower! Hello, Suzy? Suzy, are you there? This is Pete in the studio."

"Hello, Pete! This is Suzy, reporting live from the sleepover at the church tower!"

"So – how's it going there so far, Suzy?"

"Well, we've all arrived and we're just settling in. It's going to be a great evening, isn't it everyone?" Suzy encouraged everyone to answer her.

"YES!" they all shouted enthusiastically.

"Are we going to have a good time?" Suzy asked them.

"YES!"

"So," Suzy approached Charly with her microphone, "what sort of things are we going to be doing here this evening?"

"Having a midnight feast!" Charly replied. "We've all brought our own picnic stuff –

so there's loads to eat and drink."

"And what's your name?" Suzy asked.

"Charly," she replied. "Charly Fisher."

"Thanks, Charly. Now who are you?" Suzy asked, moving across the room.

"Jack Morgan! Can I say hello to all my mates?"

"You just have!" Suzy laughed. "So what else is going to happen here tonight?"

"We've got to make sure the ghosts don't get my sister!" Jack looked sneakily across at Meg.

Meg poked her tongue out at her brother – it was the only thing she could do when she wasn't able to answer back.

"Do you really believe there are ghosts here then?" Suzy asked.

"Course there are!" Nick butted in.

"Well, Pete," said Suzy. "On that spooky note, I think it's time we went back to you in the studio!"

"*Do you think you'll still be there later?*" Pete laughed.

"If the ghosts haven't got us first – you bet! We'll speak to you again in a couple of hours."

Suzy closed the live link and thanked everyone.

"Right then, guys," Danny said. "What shall we do next?"

Chapter 8

"Let's play charades!" someone suggested.

"OK – sounds cool to me," agreed Danny. "Who's going to go first?"

One of the older boys put his hand up and Danny asked him to begin. It was hilarious! It turned out that the film he had chosen to mime was *Cats and Dogs*, which should have been really simple, but no one could guess it! So one of the girls had a go and this time everyone guessed that she was miming the latest Robbie Williams hit. The Glitter Girls decided that they would act theirs together and chose to do *My Fair Lady* which was a play currently showing at the local theatre. Hannah's mum had done the costumes for it and the Glitter Girls had been lucky enough to go along and see it.

Much to Meg's irritation, Jack guessed the answer. But that didn't stop everyone from having a good time. By the time everyone had had a go, the moon had risen fully and moonlight was streaming across the churchyard outside.

"Can someone draw the curtains for me?" Danny asked.

Charly was closest to one of the windows so she hopped up to oblige. As she looked out of the window she could see the long, eerie shadows of the gravestones caused by the moonlight. Suddenly, a bird – or was it a bat? – flew straight past the window, making her jump.

"Argh!" she squealed, closing the curtains quickly.

"Are you OK?" Danny asked.

"Sure," Charly fibbed. "A bird flew past and gave me a fright." She sat down quickly and was glad to see that one of the other members of the Energy Zone had drawn the curtains at the other window.

"Anyone hungry?" Danny asked, rubbing his own stomach.

"ME!" said Jack and Nick simultaneously.

Everyone laughed, but they all agreed that a little snack wouldn't be something they wanted to miss out on. Everyone fetched the goodies they had brought and spread all the food out on a picnic rug. It was some feast! Everyone tucked in and started chatting to friends.

The Glitter Girls looked at each other and smiled.

"Isn't this cool?" Charly asked her friends.

"Brilliant!" agreed Meg.

Suddenly Flo gasped. "What was that?" she whispered. "I heard a noise! On the stairs outside!"

The Glitter Girls were sitting not far from the door to the staircase.

"Don't be daft!" said Zoe, still embarrassed about how silly she'd been earlier. "I'm sure you just imagined it."

A moment later there was a faint creak from the other side of the door. This time, the others heard it too.

"Oh!" said Charly, gripping Hannah's arm. "Did you hear that?"

"Danny!" Meg pleaded, looking puzzled.

"What?" Danny asked. "Did you hear a noise?"

"Out there!" Zoe said. "There was a creak!"

Everyone stopped eating and looked over towards the Glitter Girls and the door. There was another much louder creak – and then another one! Even Jack looked nervous.

"What do you think it is?" Hannah asked.

"I'm not sure," Danny said, gulping his last mouthful of food and standing up.

Slowly, trying to look confident, Danny went over to the door. There was another creak from outside! This time it was really loud!

"Hello?" Danny called out. "Who's there?" The moon had slipped behind a cloud and outside it was pitch black. Everything – apart from the creaking on the stairs – was silent. Danny reached over, grabbed the door handle and pulled the door open with a start.

"*Arggh!*" Danny screamed. The Glitter Girls screamed! Everyone else in the room screamed!

"My goodness, you made me jump opening the door like that!" came a voice. There on the landing outside clutching her pyjamas and sleeping bag was the vicar!

"*I* made *you* jump!" Danny laughed.

Everyone in the room was giggling with relief that the ghostly creaking was none other than the Reverend Margaret.

"Who on earth did you think I was?" Margaret laughed and entered the room. "A ghost?"

There was more laughter. "Actually,"

explained Danny, "we did! Well, who else would be climbing the church tower at this time of the night? What are you doing here?"

"Well first of all, I'm here because you left the door unlocked downstairs!" Margaret said.

"Oops!" Danny put his hand up to his mouth. "Sorry. . ."

Everyone giggled. Danny was so laid-back about things that it was difficult for anyone to get cross with him.

"And secondly," said Margaret, "I just heard you all on the radio and it sounded as if you were all having such a good time, so I thought I'd join you!" Margaret gazed at the midnight feast spread out on the floor. "And it looks like I've arrived at just the right time, doesn't it?"

"Go Glitter!" agreed the Glitter Girls, and everyone else cheered as well. Danny handed Margaret a paper plate and everyone returned to eating their very early midnight feast!

★ ♥ ★ ♥ ★ ♥ ★

"So what are we going to do next?" Suzy asked, looking at her watch when everyone had had enough to eat. "I promised to do another broadcast in about forty minutes."

"Let's do some singing!" Meg called out, looking at her own watch to discover it was gone ten o'clock.

"Singing's for babies!" Nick sniffed and the other bigger boys nodded their agreement.

"Not karaoke!" said Suzy, diving in to one of the many large bags that she'd brought with her. "Can someone help me get this lot sorted?"

"Me!" said all the Glitter Girls at once, springing up to help.

Everyone was curious to see what Suzy was on about. How could they do karaoke in the tower room, they wondered? But they soon found out. After a few minutes, Suzy asked Flo to turn out the lights. She flicked a switch and suddenly the words of a song were projected on to a wall!

"Hey!" said Flo. "Those are the words to 'Can't Get You Out of My Head'!"

"And this," said Suzy, flicking another switch, "is the music to go with it!"

The karaoke had begun!

Chapter 9

"*So is everything still cool over there in the church?*" Pete enquired.

"It certainly is, Pete!" Suzy replied. She was making her second live broadcast from the sleepover. She had decided to do it while everyone was still singing. "As you can here from the noise, we're having a great time here!"

"*So the ghosts haven't got you yet, then?*"

"No way!" Suzy laughed. "So Pete, tell me, how are we doing with our sponsorship for tonight? Supporting the mayoress's charity for the African hospital is such a good cause, we need all the money we can get!"

"*Sure, Suzy! Well we've had lots of phone calls to the station this evening, promising even more* money. *And lots of people have said that if you manage to last until tomorrow morning, they'll double their sponsorship!"*

While she was still broadcasting, Suzy asked everyone in the tower room to quieten down so that she could tell them Pete's good news. Most of them hadn't heard it because they had been too busy singing! There was a very loud cheer of approval from all of them and, back in the studio, Pete laughed.

"Well it sounds like you are still having fun! It's pretty late now, Suzy – are you lot thinking of getting any sleep?"

It was past eleven o'clock, but everyone in the tower room booed in disapproval of the idea. "Well, we might if we get the time," Suzy laughed.

"Goodnight then, Suzy and everyone at the Energy Zone sleepover!" Pete called. *"Chris is doing the breakfast show in the morning and she'll be looking forward to speaking to you then to find*

out how the rest of the night goes!"

Suzy flicked some switches and ended the live link to the radio station. The Energy Zone sleep-over was on its own again.

After some drinks, Danny started to tell everyone about a camping trip he'd been on when he was in the Scouts. He said they'd made up this long tale and everyone had had to add a bit to help keep it going. It sounded really cool and Flo asked if they could do the same thing tonight.

"Don't you lot ever want to go to sleep?" Danny laughed.

It was getting colder and some of the boys and girls had already climbed into their sleeping bags to keep warm.

"Listen," said Danny. "Let's go in groups to the loos to change into our sleeping stuff and then we can all get back here for some storytelling."

There was much giggling and excitement as

everyone did as Danny suggested. The loos were all the way down the stairs and across the other side of the church so there was a real kerfuffle as people went up and down stairs in their groups. But, half an hour later, everyone was back in the tower room.

Then the storytelling began and everyone took it in turns, just like Danny had explained. They'd turned out the lights and just had torches and a few candles to make it all the more atmospheric. Every time the story got round to Jack and Nick they started to talk about ghosts and bats and rats. It was silly but everyone laughed anyway.

Outside the only light was from the moon and every now and then, there was a faint tap on the tower room windows as a bat flickered past. But everyone knew exactly what the noise was and no one was scared. It was well gone midnight by the time the story was finished. Not long after, the tower room was quiet . . .

everyone had finally fallen asleep. So Danny blew out the candles and shone his torch around the room to make sure that everyone was where they should be, and then went to sleep himself.

★ ♥ ★ ♥ ★ ♥ ★

Charly woke with a start. She sat up and it took her a short while to work out where she was in the unfamiliar surroundings of the tower room. The moon was full and its bright light shone through the window and across the room, helping her to get her bearings.

It was cold and Charly shivered before she snuggled back down into her sleeping bag, not at all sure what had made her wake in the first place. From the comfort of her sleeping bag, Charly pushed a little button on her pink bubble watch, which illuminated the face. It was four o'clock in the morning! All around her, the other boys and girls were sleeping. Everything was still and silent, except for the loud snoring that was coming from Danny – or was it from the Reverend Margaret?

Charly sniggered to herself and closed her eyes, trying to get back to sleep. But before she could, she heard something. With her eyes shut tight and her heart thumping inside her chest, Charly hoped that she'd just imagined it. But there was the noise again! It was a creaking noise – just like the one they'd heard earlier when Margaret had turned up. Only this time it was a creaking noise in the middle of the night! And it was coming from the staircase of a church that was empty except for everyone who was sleeping in the tower room with her.

Creeeaaak!

Charly heard it again! What could she do? No one else was awake! Terrified and hardly daring to open her eyes, Charly peeked her head silently above her sleeping bag and opened one eye. She could just see Meg, fast asleep in her sleeping bag next to her. Charly wriggled closer to her in her sleeping bag.

"Charly? Charly, are you awake?"

Charly jumped as she was tapped on the shoulder by Nick.

"What is it?" Charly hissed, by now sitting bolt upright and alarmed.

"Jack went down to the loo ages ago. He hasn't come back. I think something's happened to him!"

"Have you told Danny?" Charly asked, still whispering.

"No – er, er, I, um, didn't want to wake him," Nick explained.

Charly began to wonder if this was the trick that Meg had warned them about.

"Pssst! Meg! Wake up!" she whispered, shaking Meg's sleeping bag.

Meg eventually roused.

"Whassup?" she asked, rubbing the sleep from her eyes.

By the time Charly had explained, Meg was as fully awake as her friend. Between them they quickly awoke the remaining Glitter Girls and explained what was happening.

Mooooaaannn!

There was a noise. It was coming from the other side of the doorway.

"Jack?" Meg asked quietly.

The Glitter Girls huddled closer together in the moonlit room and gave each other knowing winks.

"What do you think it is? It can't be Margaret this time," Hannah hissed, pretending to sound scared.

"Is that you, Jack?" asked Zoe in mock fear.

The Glitter Girls looked around the room.

Mooooooaaaannnn!

Jack was being very melodramatic out there on the landing. Meg tried to stiffle a giggle.

"We ought to tell the grown-ups!" Flo pleaded with Nick.

"NO! It'll be all right," Nick whispered, beginning to look a bit worried.

Mooooooooooooaaaaannnn!

Jack's moaning outside was getting louder. Was he beginning to wonder when the girls were going to get round to opening the door so he could scare them?

"Do you think the ghost has got Jack?" Nick hissed desperately.

"Oh no! Do you think . . . he's all right?" Flo put her hands to her face in horror.

"Hmm!" Meg said, suddenly appearing to become very brave and standing up. "I think I know exactly what that noise is!"

Chapter 10

In the moonlit tower room, Nick was confused. How come Meg was being so brave?

Carefully, so as not to wake anyone (and to surprise Jack as much as she possibly could), Meg tiptoed quietly across to the door. All the while, Jack continued with his agonizing groans outside. It was a wonder that no one else had woken to hear them.

Almost in silence, Meg managed to carefully turn the door handle with her right hand as she held her tiny pocket torch in her left.

"What are you doing?" Nick hissed, frightened that Jack wasn't going to be pleased with him. After all, this wasn't really going to plan.

Mooooooaaaaaannnnnnnnn!

"Got you!" Meg called, yanking open the tower room door and shining her torch right into Jack's face.

"Aaarrgggh!" he screamed, far more scared than anyone else.

"What's going on?" cried Suzy, sitting up in her sleeping bag.

"What?" Danny rubbed his eyes, trying to see in the darkness.

Soon everyone in the room was awake and panicking. Danny shone his torch around the room.

"Who's there?" he asked, storming across towards the door and flicking the light switch on.

There, at the top of the stairs, stood a very embarrassed Jack.

"What are you up to?" Danny demanded.

"Is there a problem?" Margaret asked.

"Yes!" said Meg. "My brother and his friend! They were trying to spook us!"

"What did they do?" asked Suzy, climbing out of her sleeping bag.

"I think these two are the graveyard ghosts that we've been hearing about for the last two weeks!" Hannah explained, relieved that that was all they were!

"Well – now you've woken *everyone* up just because of some stupid prank. What have you got to say for yourselves?" Danny demanded.

Jack and Nick apologized to everyone for waking them up and scaring them.

"We only did it to scare the Glitter Girls!" Nick pleaded.

"It was only meant to be a joke. . ." Jack mumbled, looking shamefaced at the floor.

"Hmm. . ." Danny thought for a while. "Well it wasn't very funny, was it? And it's disturbed everyone – not just your sister and her friends. You are a pair of twits!"

Jack and Nick apologized again.

Danny turned round and spoke to everyone

else. "OK, we can all calm down now and get back into our sleeping bags. Lights out again; and let's hope we can all get back to sleep!"

Everyone snuggled back down again. Meg didn't say anything to her brother. She just giggled quietly to herself inside the warmth of her sleeping bag, pleased that the Glitter Girls had managed to outwit her brother and his friend.

Meg could hear the gentle breathing of everyone around her as they soon fell deep into slumber again. She was determined not to go back to sleep herself though.

"Charly?" she whispered almost silently, a short while later, leaning over towards her friend. "Are you awake?"

"Yes!" she hissed in reply.

"So am I!" whispered Hannah. "What's up?"

"Wake the other two!" urged Meg. "Only don't disturb anyone else!"

Soon, all five of the Glitter Girls were awake

and huddled together. They were having one of their meetings – only by moonlight this time!

"I was just thinking," said Meg, "about how we can get our own back on Jack and Nick!"

"How?" Charly wanted to know, delighted at the thought of scaring the two boys as much as they'd scared her.

"But if we spook them, we'll wake everyone else," whispered Hannah.

"Yes," agreed Zoe. "Then we'll be in trouble, too!"

"I've got a better idea than that!" Meg hissed conspiratorially. "We could do something now that would give us revenge in the morning!"

"What's that?" Flo wanted to know.

"Remember I told you about the tricks my mum hid? Well I've got some sneezing and some itching powder in my backpack. For a start, we could put the itching stuff in the boys' trainers!"

"Nice one!" giggled Zoe, already picturing

the two boys with very itchy feet the next morning.

"Tell you what else we could do!" suggested Charly. "I brought some extra hairclips and things in case we got the chance to do some makeovers. Why don't we stick a few of my most sparkly, fluffy, girly clips in Nick's and Jack's hair? They'll wake up looking like a right pair of idiots!"

The Glitter Girls giggled as quietly as they could at the thought of seeing the two boys the next morning.

"Come on," said Zoe. "Let's get going!"

Silently, the Glitter Girls crept about the tower room. Meg got out the packets of powder and Hannah helped her to sprinkle it in the boys' shoes.

In the meantime, Flo acted as lookout as Charly and Zoe sneaked over to fetch the hair accessories from Charly's backpack. To their horror, there was a loud creak as they stepped across the sleeping bags. All the Glitter Girls froze! But no one stirred and soon after Charly and Zoe had managed to clip the boys' hair gently into stupid-looking topknots. They'd used butterfly clips and purple feathered hairgrips. Meg couldn't resist sprinkling just a little bit of the sneezing powder on their pillows as well.

The Glitter Girls settled cosily back down into their sleeping bags. In the moonlight, they could see the boys' ridiculous hairstyles. . . !

"Go Glitter!" the five girls whispered as they lay down and tried to go back to sleep.

"Aaaatchoooo!" Nick woke everyone with an enormous sneeze.

"Well, good morning!" Danny said, rousing and sitting up. He took one look at Nick's sticking-up hair and laughed. "Well – you've been framed!"

"What?" Nick asked and then burst into sneezes again.

"Aaaaaaaaatchooooo!" It was Jack's turn to wake up. "What's the time?" He went to scatch his head and felt something very strange on his head. "Aaaargh! What's this?" he said, pulling a particularly pretty large pink sparkly hairclip from his hair.

Pretty soon, everyone in the tower room was awake and giggling at the sight of the two boys. From the looks of guilty pleasure on the Glitter Girls' faces, it didn't take long for everyone to guess who had managed to get revenge on Jack and Nick. The boys were desperately trying to pull all their hair accessories off before anyone else could start making fun of them.

"Well done, girls!" Suzy winked at them. "Someone needed to teach them a lesson after last night's disturbance!"

"I'll get you for this!" Jack warned Meg, slipping on his trainers.

Charly couldn't help but giggle at the thought of the itching that was to come his way later that morning.

"There's no time for that!" Danny laughed. "We've got one more broadcast to go! Come on, everyone – let's get dressed and ready for action!"

Suzy was already busy connecting to the radio station and soon everyone was up and ready, sleeping bags packed away. It was time to go on air.

". . .And now we're going to join the gang from the Energy Zone who have been sleeping over in the church tower. Hello, Suzy?"

"Good morning from the church tower room, Chris!" Suzy replied.

"Good morning to you! And how is it going there? Did you all sleep well?"

"Well," Suzy looked around the room at everyone and smiled. "We did sleep, didn't we?"

"Yessss!" everyone cheered.

"But we did have a few bumps and noises in the night!" Suzy said, and she went on to explain to Chris what had happened.

Chris found it all very amusing. "So can you tell us how much we've managed to raise with our sleepover, Chris?" Suzy enquired.

"Of course! We've just tried to tot it up and reckon that it's close to four hundred pounds! So well done to everyone from Energy Zone, and a big thank you to all our listeners!"

"So, Danny," Suzy turned to the Energy Zone's leader. "If we add that to the money that you've already raised I think that makes over five hundred pounds, doesn't it?"

"It certainly does, Suzy! And all for the mayoress's charity to buy new and much needed equipment for the children's hospital in Africa."

"Well, that's wonderful – everyone should be really proud of his or her achievement! Chris –

we'll say goodbye for now! We're all feeling hungry and could do with something to eat!"

"Byeeeee!" the boys and girls all called.

As Suzy switched off her radio equipment and everyone gathered up the last of their stuff, the Glitter Girls hugged each other, pleased that they had been part of this adventure.

"Right!" said the Reverend Margaret, looking around at everyone. "Who's for breakfast in the church hall? My husband said he'd cook for us."

There was a cheer of approval all round.

As they all trooped down the stairs, Meg saw her brother stop to scratch his foot inside his trainers. She smiled at the Glitter Girls and nodded towards Jack.

Hannah stifled a yawn. "Well – we didn't get that much sleep did we?"

"No – but it was a great sleepover," said Flo.

"A spooky sleepover, you mean," laughed Charly.

"Some spooks, though!" exclaimed Zoe, pointing at Nick and Jack.

"But it was a great adventure, wasn't it?" Meg asked her best friends.

Just then, Jack let out an enormous sneeze! The Glitter Girls couldn't help laughing.

"One of our best yet!" suggested Hannah.

"Go Glitter!" the others all agreed. And they followed the boys towards breakfast!

Don't miss:

Christmas Crackers

It's Christmas, the Glitter Girls' favourite time of year, and this year's going to be extra-special!

The girls have heard about something REALLY cool – there's a pantomime at the local theatre and they need extras. It's a dream come true! The Glitter Girls have GOT to win parts, and get the chance to meet the glamorous leading lady. . .